Praise for Storyshares

"One of the brightest innovators and game-changers in the education industry."
— Forbes

"Your success in applying research-validated practices to promote literacy serves as a valuable model for other organizations seeking to create evidence-based literacy programs."
— Library of Congress

"We need powerful social and educational innovation, and Storyshares is breaking new ground. The organization addresses critical problems facing our students and teachers. I am excited about the strategies it brings to the collective work of making sure every student has an equal chance in life."
— Teach For America

"It's the perfect idea. There's really nothing like this. I mean, wow, this will be a wonderful experience for young people."
— Andrea Davis Pinkney, Executive Director, Scholastic

"Reading for meaning opens opportunities for a lifetime of learning. Providing emerging readers with engaging texts that are designed to offer both challenges and support for each individual will improve their lives for years to come. Storyshares is a wonderful start."
— David Rose, Co-founder of CAST & UDL

Storyshares presents

Published by Storyshares, LLC

Storyshares
Storyshares, LLC
24 N. Bryn Mawr Avenue #340
Bryn Mawr, Pennsylvania 19010-3304
www.storyshares.org

Inspiring reading with a new kind of book.

Interest Level: Middle School
Grade Level Equivalent: 2.6

ISBN 9798885978446
Book design by Saskia Globig

The Sea Warriors of Sunken Ships

Margaret Connors

Storyshares

Contents

Chapter One

I wake up and put on my wetsuit to go scuba diving. I get that tingle of excitement in my neck and stomach. We will be exploring some shipwrecks in Lake Superior today.

I love Lake Superior, so cold and blue and mysterious. I love it for water skiing and swimming and especially for scuba diving.

One of my dad's Coast Guard buddies, Ray, asked if his son could go with us today. He's older than me. I've seen him around school.

He's Native American and kinda cute. Plays football. His name's Jared.

I don't think he knows who I am.

Chapter Two

Jared wants to get better at diving, so Dad's going to work with him.

I'll probably get stuck babysitting my little brother Peter most of the day, though. What a drag.

He's not real little. He's ten, but I'll have to watch him inside the ships.

If Mom were here, if Mom...

And back comes that pressure in my chest, and my throat tightens, and my eyes sting.

There's a knock on my door. It's Dad.

"How're you doing this morning, Kaylee?" he asks.

I can't even talk. The tears just spill over. Dad puts his arms around me and lets me cry.

He says quietly, "I've been having a rough morning missing her too. Diving will be good for us today. How about if you get some breakfast going?"

That was Mom's job too, I think to myself. But I do it, just like cleaning the bathrooms.

Oh, never mind. We are going diving today.

Chapter Three

So, shortly after, we are on the boat and in the water. We have new waterproof microphones. Now we can communicate and hear each other's conversations.

"Kaylee," says Dad, "I'm getting a low reading on Peter's oxygen. Go adjust his tank."

I don't know why, I just snapped. "Why do I always have to take care of my little brother? Since Mom died, you keep dumping more on me."

Dad jumps in the water. He adjusts Peter's tank himself and says, "How's that, Sweet Pete?"

Peter says, "Don't give me too much or I'll look like a blowfish."

"Kaylee," Dad says, "losing Mom has been hard on all of us. We have to pull together more now."

"I wanted to go to the movies with my friends today," I say. And suddenly I blurt out, "I wish I wasn't part of this family!"

Dad says soothingly, "We're going to get through this, honey. Let's help each other. This is Peter's first independent dive. Let's make it fun for him."

There is a pause as Dad climbs back on the boat.

Dad continues, "Ready? Peter, this ship is the *Kiowa*. It's a freight steamer that sank in 1929 in a windstorm. Do you see the enclosed ladderway? Go ahead and climb down it."

"Wow!" says Peter. "This is awesome! Look at this tunnel down here! Can we go in it?"

"You sure can," says Dad.

We swim through with a school of fish.

"Look at the end of the tunnel, Peter," says Jared. "It's the propeller shaft."

"Wow! It's huge! Those gears are enormous!" says Peter.

Dad chuckles, watching us explore.

The phone crackles with an incoming call.

"It's Ray, from Coast Guard. Bad winds coming in. There'll be turbulence. Take cover."

"Thanks, Ray." Dad clicks off the phone.

"Kids, Jared, that was your dad. All of you get back into the ladderway. Try to secure yourselves around the ladder. Stay in the enclosure. The storm should be over quickly."

Swimming back is difficult as the water begins churning.

At the ladderway, Jared pushes Peter upward. "Hang on, Buddy." Jared turns to help me.

As I step higher, there is sudden suction. It pulls Peter up and out of the enclosure.

"Something's got me!" he yells.

Jared grabs for him, but Peter is snatched away.

Chapter Four

Jared and I both bolt out and search frantically in the chaotic water.

Suddenly we see an unbelievable sight: a hideous serpent with the horned head of a lynx. It's carrying Peter by the scruff of the neck.

"Help me!" cries Peter.

The big creature looks at us with burning, evil eyes, then lurches into the murky waters. Horrified, we torpedo ourselves after it and hunt desperately. But we can't find Peter again.

After a long search, Jared is exhausted. He finally says, "We're almost out of oxygen. We have to go up."

"NO!" I yell. "We can't leave without Peter!"

Jared grabs me firmly by the hand. "We'll drown if we don't."

I guess he's right, but I'm so frightened for Peter. We swim toward the surface as the water calms.

"We're coming up, Dad," I say into the mic, but there's no answer.

When we break the surface of the water, we see Dad lying face down on the deck.

Next to him is a heavy rope. The winds must have blown it down. It looks like it hit him in the back of the head.

"Dad, what happened?" I ask, kneeling down to him.

There's still no answer.

Chapter Five

"He's breathing and has a pulse," says Jared as he checks him.

"I'll call my father."

I am trying not to panic. But Peter... and Dad...

Jared contacts his father at the Coast Guard and tells him what happened.

"I'm on my way," says Ray.

Before too long, a Coast Guard helicopter reaches the boat and hovers over us. Ray is inside, along with the pilot and several other people.

A team climbs down a ladder and checks out Dad and us kids. They put Dad on a stretcher and lift him aboard.

Ray comes down the ladder and stays with us as the helicopter flies to shore.

"What happened to Peter?" asks Ray.

"I'm not sure what I saw," says Jared, "but Peter got swept away underwater."

"By a huge snake with the head of a big cat! Like out of a horror story!" I say.

"Did it have horns?" asks Ray.

"Yeah, it did," says Jared. "How did you know?"

Jared and I both stare at his father.

Chapter Six

"It sounds like the Sea Lynx of Lake Superior. My grandmother talks about it. She's Ojibwa Indian and calls the creature Mishipeshu."

He pronounces clearly for me: mi-ship'-a-shoo.

"She describes it just like you did," Ray adds.

"You never told me this," says Jared.

"It never came up, son. And you wouldn't have believed it anyway. My grandmother gave me these for protection."

Ray unties a leather cord he has around his neck. On it hang three birds' talons, giant claws, made of copper.

"They say these are from thunderbirds, spirit

birds sent by the gods to protect the Ojibwa people. Thunderbirds have power over Mishipeshu.

"Let's each of us take one of these and go
look for Peter."

Chapter Seven

"Where do we even start to look?" I ask. "Where would a sea lynx go? Would it have eaten Peter? Did he drown? Lake Superior is huge. How will we ever find him? "

"I have tracking equipment that should work with your communication system. When was the last time you heard from him?" asks Ray.

"It's been almost an hour," says Jared.

"An hour?" says Ray. "Hmm. Let's try to reach him." Ray connects his device.

I speak into it, "Peter, can you hear me? It's Kaylee. Are you there?"

A groggy, weak voice comes back. "Hello? Is

that you, Kaylee? I'm in a cave, on a shelf in the rocks."

Ray says, "Keep talking, Peter. I'm tracking the source of your call."

"Are you hurt?" I ask.

"Not too much," answers Peter.

"Kaylee, drive the boat," says Ray. "The signal is coming from the east. Head to that wall of rocks."

"Oh, Ray, that's where Mom had the boating accident. She died there. I don't want to go. You two go."

Ray says, "Kaylee, you need to be stronger than your feelings. We have to find Peter as quickly as possible. Jared, drive.

"We're coming for you, Peter. Can you see the boat?" asks Ray.

"I can," says Peter. "But I can't get out. The sea monster..." There is a low growl through Peter's mic.

"Are we getting closer?" asks Jared.

"Yes," says Peter, "but the opening is really skinny. You can't see me."

"Yell at us!" says Jared.

Peter does, and the sea monster shoots upright like a king cobra, covering the vertical opening.

My stomach drops.

Chapter Eight

"There!" yells Ray, pointing to its scaly back.

Jared speeds the boat to the crevice and leaps onto Mishipeshu's back. Jared wraps his arms and legs around the monster.

He grabs the hair between its horns and yanks its head backward.

Yowling, crying out in anger and pain, Mishipeshu twists and writhes.

Then it goes underwater, trying to shake Jared off. But Jared rides it like a bucking bronco.

With the crevice wide open, I call, "Peter, come out!

"I can't! I'm trapped in some rocks!" yells Peter.

The monster surfaces again then takes a surprise jolt backwards. The motion slams Jared's air tanks into the canyon wall. They get crushed.

Jared is knocked out. Mishipeshu throws itself onto Jared's body and pushes him underwater.

"No!" I scream. "Come back!"

Chapter Nine

Ray and I are stunned. We wait, gripping the sides of the boat.

Neither Jared nor the monster surface. I totally lose it and start crying hysterically.

Ray puts his hands firmly on my shoulders and speaks urgently. "You are the only one small enough to get in through the crevice to save Peter. Go now, while the sea monster is distracted."

I stop crying and gulp.

"Go now!" says Ray.

I climb onto the rock ledge, then run toward the opening and try to squeeze through it.

As I squeeze in, rocks from above crumble and fall around me.

One opens a nest of brown bats. Squealing, beady-eyed, and hairy, they fly into my face.

Screaming, I try to knock them away. But with scratching claws and bony wings, the attack continues.

With my arms flailing and fighting, I bolt back towards the boat.

Chapter Ten

"Kaylee, take this!" Ray yells as he tosses me his jacket and grabs some oars. We beat off the bats until they retreat.

I start to get back in the boat when Peter hollers again, "Get me out of here!"

I stop. I am panting, sweating, heart pounding, speechless.

I can't do it... those bats...

But Peter's on the other side of those bats... Peter....

I turn back toward the cave. I pull the jacket over my head and partially cover my face.

"Take this one for Peter," says Ray, throwing me another jacket as he grips the oars.

I dash to the cave. The bats swarm me again and rocks crumble and fall.

Biting my lip, I shove myself through.

I run to Peter and throw my weight against one of the stones holding him in the cave.

It's too heavy.

A geyser, a massive waterspout, shoots water up from behind the rocks. Jared is in the water.

He's wrapped in the coil of the monster's tail.

Chapter Eleven

Looking closer, I see that he is conscious.

I throw a rock that hits Mishipishu's head, spinning it. It releases Jared.

He snatches the end of its tail, then climbs up the beast. He winds the lynx's tail around its own neck, jerking it tight.

"All choked up, Kitty Cat?" laughs Jared.

The cat's eyes bulge as it collapses in the water.

Jared jumps onto the ledge with his fists in the air in victory.

"Ray!" I yell through the crevice. "Give me one of those oars for a lever."

Ray slides it to me through the opening. I jam it between two rocks.

Jared and I push until one moves enough for Peter to slip out. Finally free! I grab Peter and hug him fiercely.

"I thought I was gonna be a sea monster sandwich!" he cries.

"No, silly. C'mon. We've got to go," I say.

The three of us squeeze through the cave's opening and run.

"Jared!" I yell, "You were GREAT!"

"And you were INCREDIBLE!" Jared yells. He picks me up, spins me around, kisses my forehead, and puts me down to keep running.

"I was incredible too," yells Peter, "but don't kiss me." We run to the boat where Ray is waiting.

We climb inside and all fall into each other's arms.

Chapter Twelve

That evening, we all go to the hospital to visit my dad. He had has a concussion and some broken bones, but he will be all right.

"You'll never believe what happened, Dad!" says Peter. "We're sending this story to Hollywood! I'm going to be the star!"

We kids tell Dad what happened that afternoon. Dad looks amused, but not sure what to think.

Mostly, he's glad that Peter is fine.

I pull out my thunderbird's talon and say, "This talon is what helped me save Peter."

"Yeah," says Jared. "I never could have fought that sea monster without mine."

"No," says Ray stepping forward. "It didn't have anything to do with good luck charms. It was your courage and love for your brother that saved Peter and tackled the sea monster."

"I'm proud of you," says Dad. "Your mother would have been too. Thanks, Jared and Ray." Dad grins. "You are the Sea Warriors of Sunken Ships."

"Yeah," says Jared. "Superheroes. That's us."

"And I am glad to be part of this family, Dad," I tell him.

And it feels good to mean it.

"I'm glad you are too," he says, reaching up to stroke my hair.

"Did you get any good pictures, Ray?" asks Peter.

"Next time," says Ray. "Next time."

About the Author

Margaret Connors is a contributing author to the Storyshares libary.

About the Publisher

Storyshares is a publisher focused on supporting the millions of teens and adults who struggle with reading by creating a new shelf in the library specifically for them. The ever-growing collection features content that is compelling and culturally relevant for teens and adults, yet still readable at a range of lower reading levels.

Storyshares generates content by engaging deeply with writers, bringing together a community to create this new kind of book. With more intriguing and approachable stories to choose from, the teens and adults who have fallen behind are improving their skills and beginning to discover the joy of reading.

For more information, visit storyshares.org.

Easy to Read. Hard to Put Down.

www.ingramcontent.com/pod-product-compliance
Lightning Source LLC
Chambersburg PA
CBHW071230170626
46809CB00005BA/2005